Dedicated to Hannah and Luke. **J. P.**

www.thegoodartist.co.uk

Text copyright © John Place 2005
Illustrations copyright © Anthony Trimmer 2005

The moral rights of the author and illustrator have been asserted.

Printed in Spain by Zure
ISBN: 978-1-85345-424-0

The Good Artist

Written by John Place

Illustrated by Tony Trimmer

In the beginning there was a blank page.
It belonged to the Good Artist who was well known
for making perfect pictures.
He never made mistakes.

One day the Artist began to draw on the page.

He drew the sun and sky.
He drew the land and the sea.
He drew the animals, fish, birds and insects.

Then He drew Man.
When He finished, everything was perfect.
The Good Artist told Man, 'All this belongs to you.'

The Good Artist made Man a friend,
someone to help him.
She was called Woman.

One day Man and Woman broke the Artist's rule. They picked up brushes from the Forbidden Paint Pot. As soon as they disobeyed the Artist ...

... SPLAT!!!

As time went on, many people tried to draw like the Good Artist. At first they drew good things like clothes and shelter.

However, without the Artist's help and instructions, people also drew bad things like ...
... weapons.

This caused a lot of hurt and pain.

The Good Artist saw what happened to His once perfect picture. He still loved the people He had drawn. This time He drew a special instruction book to show them how to live and be kind to each other.

Some people read the instructions
and tried to follow them.
They found it hard because they were used to
drawing and doing what they wanted.

Some people didn't even believe there was an Artist! Although many read the book, only a few would follow the instructions.

This was a problem. No matter how
hard people tried, they could not
draw as well as the Artist and they certainly
couldn't rub out the mistakes they made.

The Artist had the answer and
He performed a great miracle.
He sent His only spotless Son into
the picture to show people how to live
and draw as the Artist wanted them to.

He began to rub out the mistakes people had made ...

... and because He was the
Artist's Son, He drew perfectly like His Dad.
He didn't make any mistakes.

The Artist's Son told many people all about the Good Artist and how much He loved them.

The Son told off the leaders of the people for using the instruction book to boss people around.

This made them angry.

The leaders called Him a liar. They didn't believe
He was really the Artist's Son, so they stained Him
to death because they wanted to live their own way.

But because they weren't His stains,
the Artist drew His Son again.

The Artist's Son told His followers that anyone who believed in Him must be drawn again as children of the Artist.

Then the Son returned to His Father.

When anyone believed in the Artist and the Son, they were drawn again. Now people could once again be friends with the Artist.

Those who had been drawn again told others about the Good Artist.

Many other people came back to the Artist and were drawn again.

At the very end of the Artist's picture, those who believed in His Son were taken out to live with the Artist and His family forever.

not
The End.